Jack's Worry

Sam Zuppardi

WALKER BOOKS
AND SUBSIDIARIES
LONDON · BOSTON · SYDNEY · AUCKLAND

Jack loved playing
the trumpet.

FLG

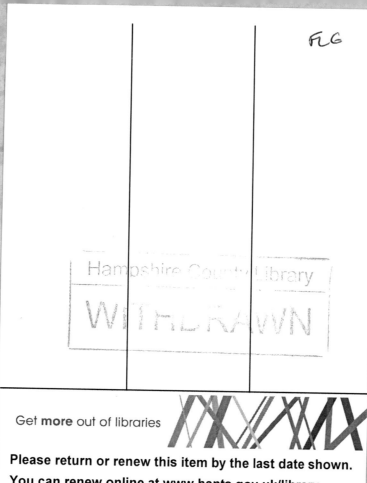

Get **more** out of libraries

Please return or renew this item by the last date shown.

You can renew online at www.hants.gov.uk/library

Or by phoning 0300 555 1387

Hampshire
County Council

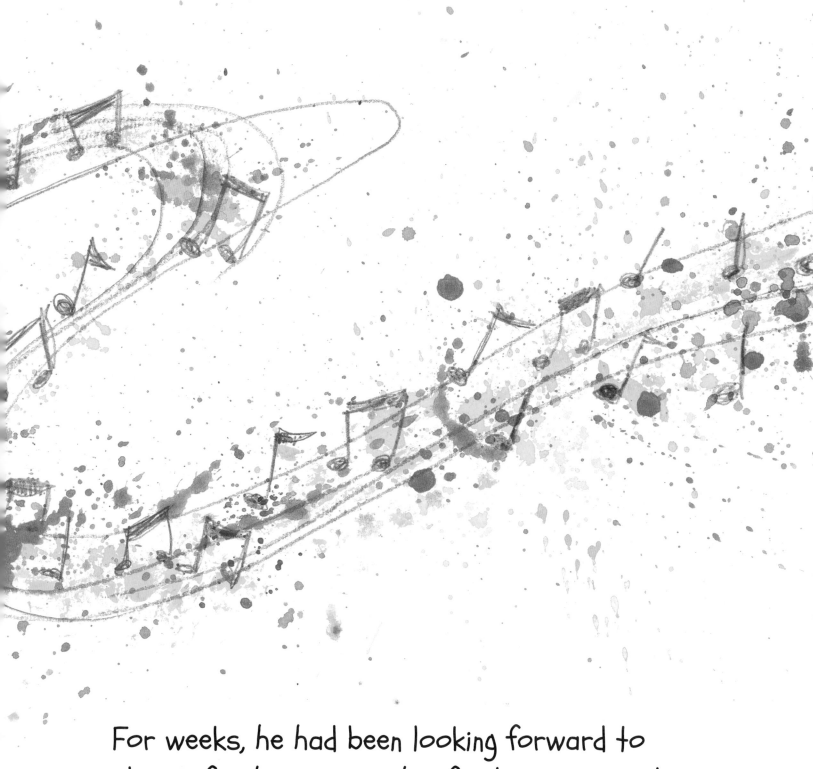

For weeks, he had been looking forward to playing for his mum in his first-ever concert.

But on the morning of the big day,
he found he had a Worry.

"Time to get up," said Jack's mum. "I've made you a special pre-concert breakfast."

Jack crawled under
the blankets.
But his Worry crawled
under with him.

Jack hid under the bed.
But his Worry followed
him there, too.

When Jack finally got downstairs, his Worry made it hard for him to eat his special breakfast.

"Everything OK?" asked his mum.

Jack wanted to tell her about his Worry,
but he couldn't find the words.

After breakfast, Jack ran
around the garden, trying
to lose his Worry.

But every time he stopped, it caught right back up with him.

So Jack did the one thing that always made him happy...

He took out his trumpet
and started to play.

But that only made things worse.

Jack's Worry was here to stay.

"It's almost time to go," Jack's mum said.

But Jack couldn't go to the concert with such a big Worry.

He couldn't do anything with such a big Worry.

Suddenly, it was all a bit too much for Jack.

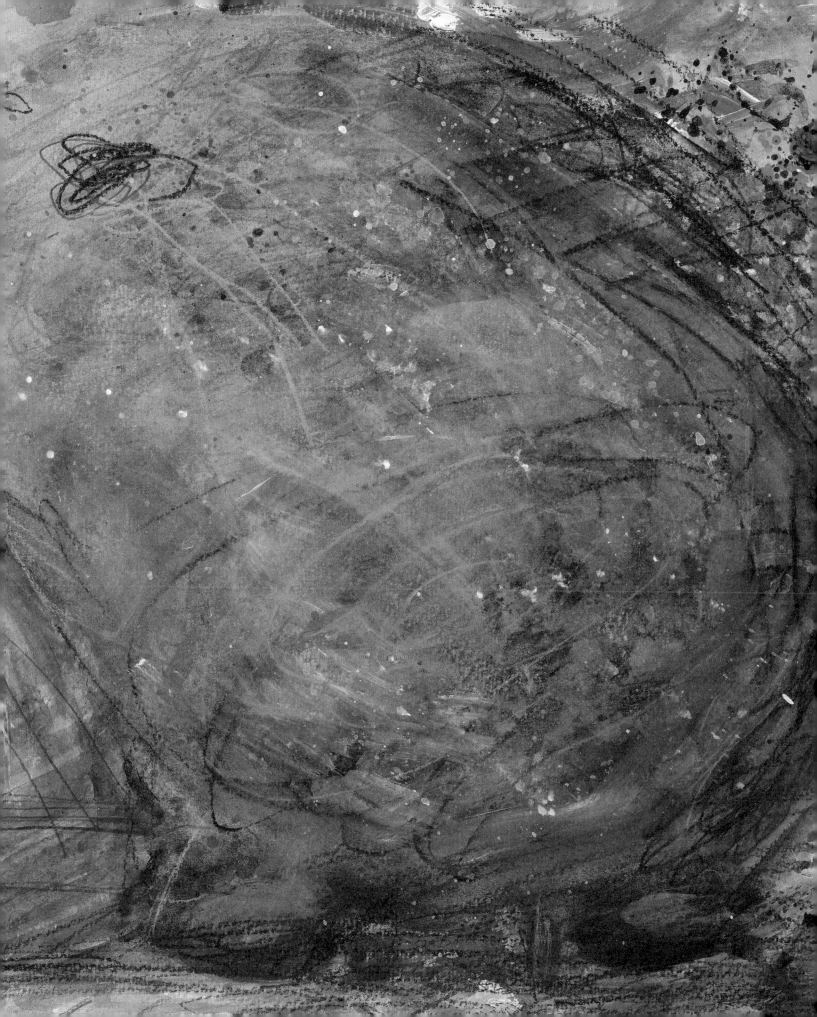

Jack's mum crouched in front of him.
"I thought you were looking forward
to today," she said.

For the first time that day,
Jack stopped trying to get rid
of his Worry. Instead, he looked
at it. Really looked at it.

And he found
the words he needed.

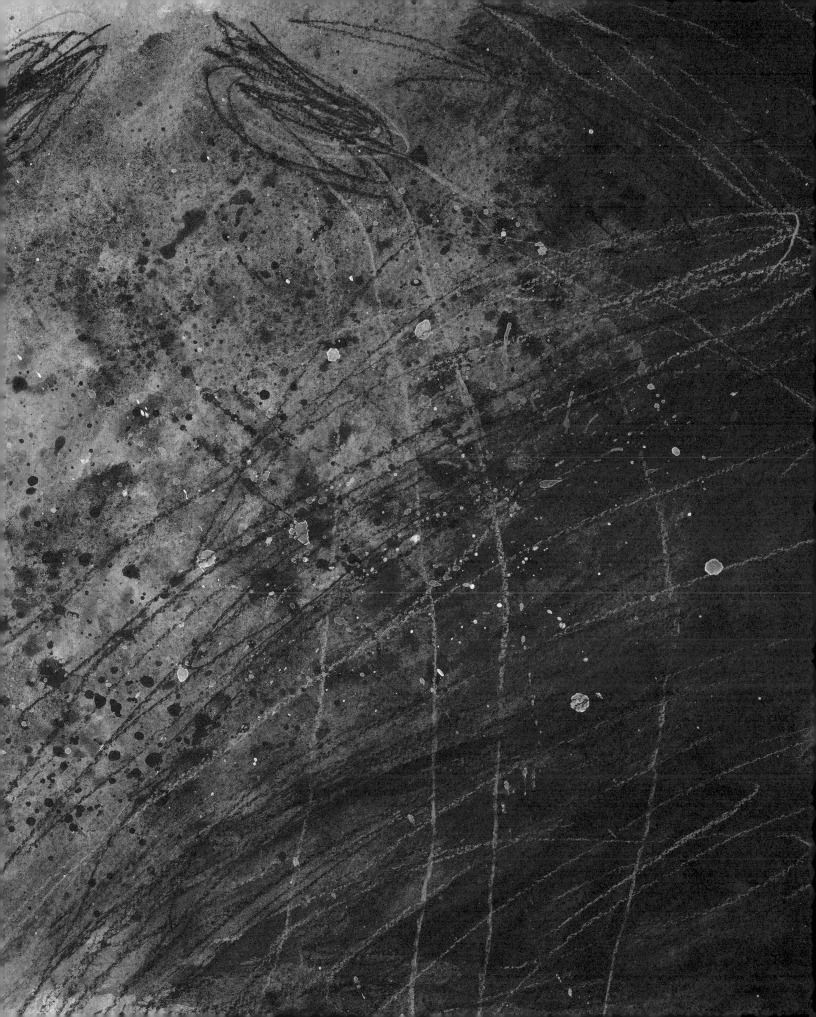

"I don't want to play in the concert!"
he told his mum.
"I'm worried I'll make a mistake
and you won't love me anymore!"

"That's quite a worry," said Jack's mum.
"I'm glad you told me. And you know what?
The concert isn't about playing perfectly.
It's about having fun and sharing something
you love with people who love you.

And I will still
love you even if
you play every
note wrong."

Suddenly Jack's Worry
wasn't so big anymore.

By the time they got to the school, his Worry was teeny-tiny.

When he saw his friends with their
Worries, he knew just what to do.

And the mistakes? There were a few –
but Jack was too busy enjoying
himself to worry.

For Luisa

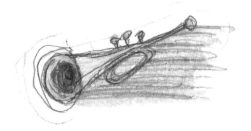

First published 2016 by Walker Books Ltd
87 Vauxhall Walk, London SE11 5HJ

2 4 6 8 10 9 7 5 3 1

This book has been typeset in Schoolbell

Printed in China

British Library Cataloguing in Publication Data:
a catalogue record for this book is available from the British Library

ISBN 978-1-4063-6779-9

www.walker.co.uk